BRILLIANT BRITS

HENRY VIII

RICHARD BRASSEY

Orion
Children's Books

Which king had six wives and chopped the heads off two of them?

Which king chopped the heads off two of his chief ministers and would have done a third if the third hadn't died before he could?

Which king said he was more important than the Pope and had all the monasteries in England pulled down?

Which king had over seventy palaces, castles and houses and still wanted more?

Henry's father was Henry VII, the first Tudor King of England. His mother, Elizabeth of York, may look familiar as the queen whose picture we still sometimes see on playing cards.

He's brilliant!
A genius!
Henry's subjects at school: Latin English French Italian Spanish Greek Maths Science Astronomy Geography Music etc. etc.
Henry was born in 1491 and started school at the age of three. He was brilliant at all his lessons.
He's brilliant!
A perfect young prince!
He was also brilliant at sports such as tennis, archery and riding. Most of all he loved jousting.

Nobody thought Henry would ever become king because he had an older brother, Arthur. But then Arthur died, making Henry heir to the throne.

Although Henry was only eleven his father said he'd better get engaged to Catherine of Aragon, who was Arthur's widow. Catherine was seventeen. She was a Spanish princess, and very well educated. She enjoyed sports and had a pet monkey. She and Henry got on famously.

Just before Henry's eighteenth birthday, his father died. Henry, who was now six foot two, married Catherine and soon afterwards they were crowned King and Queen.

People could not say enough good things about Henry. They thought he was going to be the best king ever. The coronation party lasted for eight days. There was endless jousting. Luckily Catherine seemed to enjoy it.

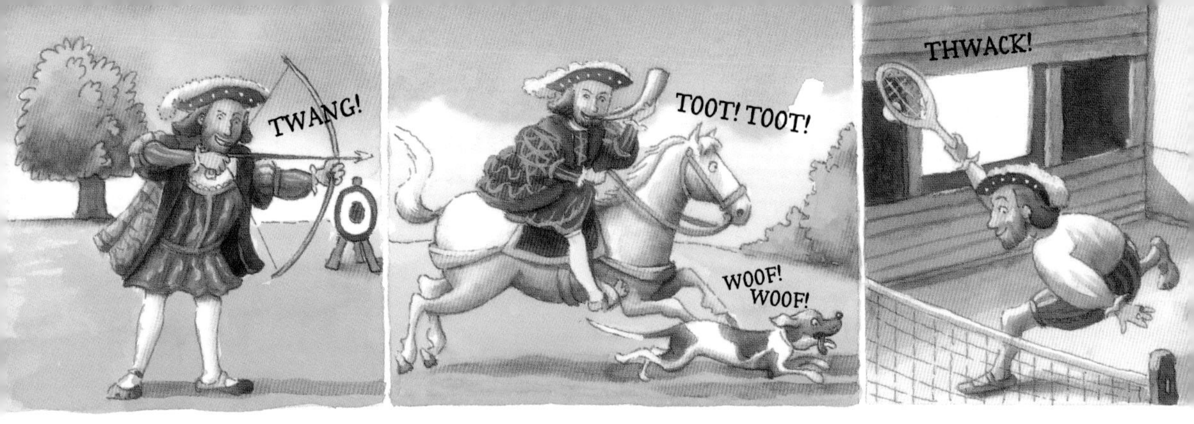

When Henry first became king, he spent all his time on fun things like archery, hunting, playing tennis, jousting, dancing, playing the lute and making up songs – though not the famous 'Greensleeves' which was written later.

Luckily he had just the man to run the country while he enjoyed himself. Cardinal Wolsey got up at four o'clock every morning and worked all day without stopping to eat or go to the toilet.

If Wolsey had to go out, he often rode on a donkey. He held a perfumed orange over his nose because in those days the streets were very smelly. On his few days off he loved nothing better than to shop for expensive items like jewellery.

The other thing he loved was building palaces. Unfortunately Henry also liked jewellery and palaces. Whenever Wolsey had something really nice, Henry wanted it for himself.

When his father died Henry inherited seven palaces, seventeen big houses and fourteen castles. By the time Henry died he owned over seventy assorted palaces, castles and big houses.

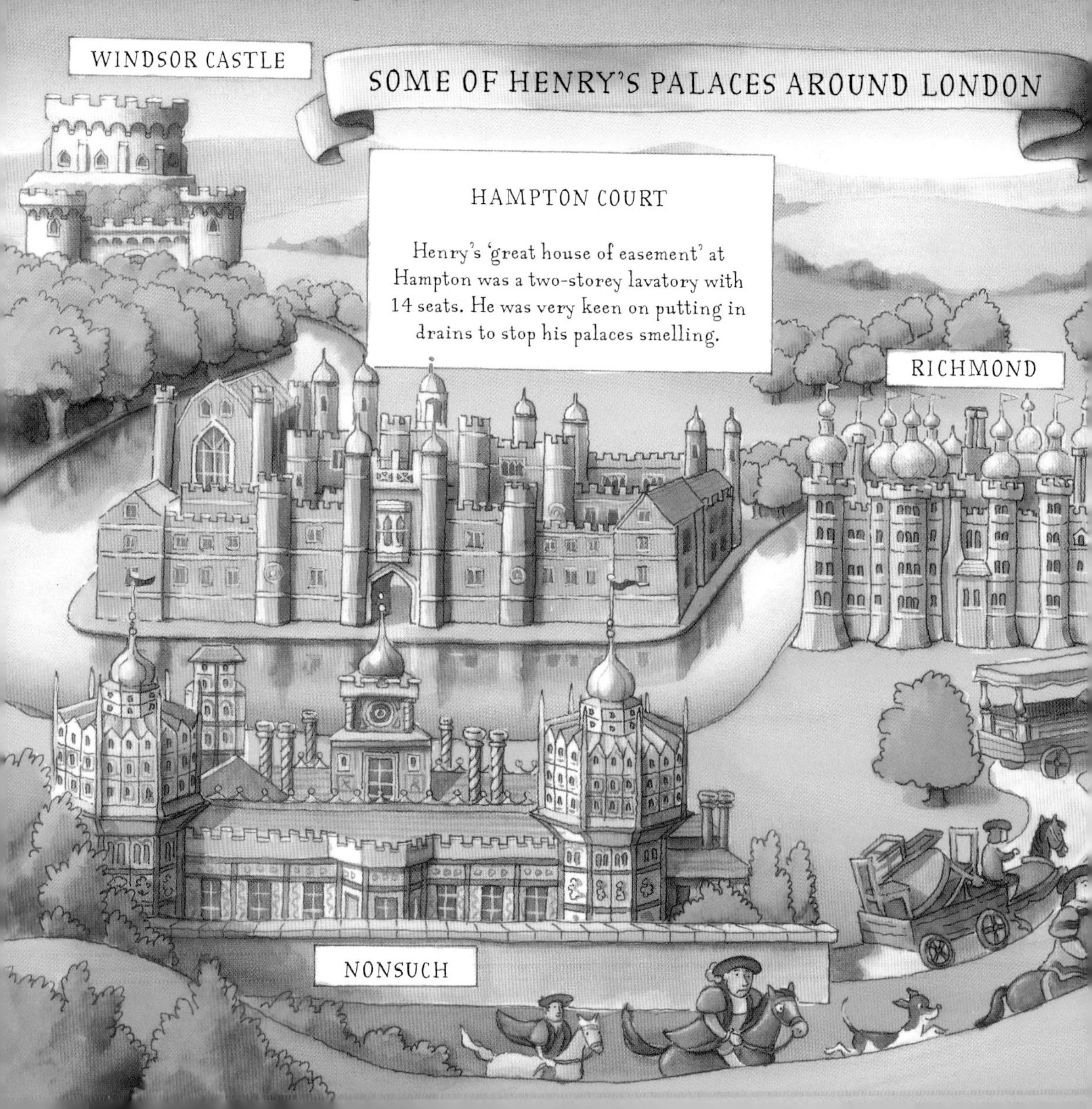
WINDSOR CASTLE
SOME OF HENRY'S PALACES AROUND LONDON
HAMPTON COURT
Henry's 'great house of easement' at Hampton was a two-storey lavatory with 14 seats. He was very keen on putting in drains to stop his palaces smelling.
RICHMOND
NONSUCH

As soon as he got bored or a palace started to smell, Henry moved to another, taking all his servants and furniture with him. This happened about every ten days.

Two of his best palaces were Whitehall and Hampton Court, which he made Cardinal Wolsey give him.

Nobody knows exactly what Henry's palace at Whitehall looked like, as it all burned down, but at one time it was the biggest palace in Europe.
Anybody smartly dressed could wander in and watch Henry having dinner. People's manners were not very good in those days so all sorts of notices had to be put up.
No nose picking
Don't breathe smelly breath on the King.
Don't wipe hands o tapestr

All Henry's meals had at least thirteen courses. One of his favourite things was jelly, moulded into wonderful shapes such as animals and castles.

It took ten men to make Henry's bed. He usually had eight mattresses. One man's job was to stick his dagger into each mattress to make sure there were no murderers hiding inside!

Every night Henry took a small piece of fur to bed. He hoped the fleas would jump on it and bite it instead of him.

Mind his toes!

ZZzzz!

Don't leave dirty dishes on the King's bed!

It was considered a great honour to sleep on a camp bed beside Henry in case he needed anything in the night.

Henry always had lots of parties. He especially enjoyed fancy dress. Once he and some friends disguised themselves as Robin Hood and his merry men. Henry thought it was very funny when Catherine pretended not to know who he was.

It was often very cold in winter. One Christmas the River Thames froze solid and the King and Queen, wrapped in furs, were able to ride across the ice from St Paul's Cathedral to Greenwich.

Henry was very jealous of Francis, the King of France, who was also tall and good at sports, but was richer than he was. He was delighted when he found out that Francis had skinny legs.

The two of them had a get-together, known as 'The Field of the Cloth of Gold' because they spent so much money showing off to each other. There were competitions and such furious jousting that Francis got a black eye and Henry sprained his wrist.

Henry often had jousting accidents. Then one day, while chasing after his hawk, he tried to pole vault a ditch. The pole snapped and he ended up stuck head first in the mud, and would have drowned if his footman hadn't pulled him out. He had had so many accidents already that people worried about him.

Henry had one big problem: he didn't have an heir. Catherine had had a daughter, but there was no son to be King after Henry. He decided he'd better get a new wife. He told Wolsey to ask the Pope if he could have a divorce . . .

The Pope said 'No!' So Henry made himself head of the Church of England, instead of the Pope. Then he gave himself a divorce. He fired Cardinal Wolsey and would have had him beheaded, but Wolsey fell ill and died.

Henry VIII is famous for having six wives. There is a rhyme which describes the fate of each one in the right order.

Divorced, beheaded, died,
Divorced, beheaded, survived!

All I want is a beautiful wife who'll give me a son . . . and agree with everything I say! Is that too much for a king to ask?

DIVORCED

CATHERINE OF ARAGON

Catherine was married to Henry for twenty-four years. She had one daughter, called Mary, and a baby son who died. Henry began to worry that God might be angry with him for marrying his dead brother's wife. After the divorce Catherine lived alone. She died before Henry.

ANNE BOLEYN

As soon as he'd divorced Catherine, Henry married Anne, who had been one of her ladies-in-waiting. After three years of marriage she only managed to have a daughter, Elizabeth. Anne argued a lot with Henry and he thought she was cheating on him, so he had her beheaded.

JANE SEYMOUR

As soon as Anne had been beheaded, Henry married Jane. Jane had been one of Anne's ladies-in-waiting. She had a son, Edward. Jane died twelve days after he was born and Henry was so upset that he didn't marry anybody for two years.

ANNE OF CLEVES

Henry's minister Cromwell showed him a painting of Anne. He liked what he saw, but when he met her he thought she was ugly and smelly. It was too late to stop the wedding and Anne was a foreign princess so he couldn't behead her. He divorced her as soon as he could and had Cromwell beheaded instead.

KATHARINE HOWARD

Katharine was one of Anne's ladies-in-waiting. She was over thirty years younger than Henry. He fell head over heels in love with her, but then he found out that she'd had secret lovers before him, so he had her beheaded.

SURVIVED

Does that feel nice, my lord?

KATHARINE PARR

Katharine number 3 was very sensible. She agreed with everything Henry said and looked after him when he was old and his leg hurt. All his children liked her and she managed to survive until after Henry died.

HENRY'S CHILDREN

EDWARD VI – King from 1547–1553

MARY – Queen from 1553–1558

ELIZABETH I –
Queen from 1558–1603

The ghosts of Henry's unhappy wives are still said to wander restlessly. Anne Boleyn leads a ghostly procession to the chapel in the Tower of London. Katharine Howard runs screaming down a passage at Hampton Court and Jane Seymour sometimes pops up there too, carrying a candle.

Before marrying Anne of Cleves, Henry saw a picture of Christina of Denmark. He thought she looked gorgeous and asked her to marry him. Christina sensibly refused but added that if she'd had two heads she would gladly have given him one.

When he made himself head of the Church of England, Henry had announced that nobody was more important than him except God. But all over the country there were monasteries full of monks who believed the Pope was more important than Henry.

Henry ordered Cromwell to pull down the monasteries and throw out the monks. The people who worked for them had to find new jobs. He left the monasteries in ruins and sold most of the land.

Henry ate a lot and as he grew older he got very large. His suits had constantly to be let out. Since it was fashionable to dress like the King, all the gentlemen at court had their suits let out too and filled them up with padding.

Henry had always enjoyed leading his army across the Channel to fight the French. By the time of his last expedition he had grown so heavy he had to be winched onto his horse.

We can see how Henry's shape changed from his suits of armour, which still survive in the Tower of London.

Something else we can see is one of Henry's finest ships. The *Mary Rose* filled with water and sank when she was on her way to fight the French. Over 600 men drowned. Henry was watching from shore and was very upset. In 1982 the wreck was rescued from the seabed and is now in Portsmouth.

In his last years one of Henry's legs became swollen and painful, which made him extremely bad-tempered. He spent most of his time shut in his bedroom, reading and mixing medicines out of worms, crushed pearls and what he believed to be dragon's blood.

Often the only person he would see was his fool, Will Somers. Will said things to Henry that nobody else would have dared to say, and made him laugh. But at the end Henry felt so ill that he didn't even want to see Will, and he died, lonely and miserable, in January 1547, aged fifty-six.